YOKAI
STORIES

CHIN MUSIC
P R E S S

YOKAI STORIES

Written by
ZACK DAVISSON

Illustrated by
ELEONORA D'ONOFRIO

CHIN MUSIC PRESS

For my amazing wife Miyuki; thanks for all the magic you bring to my world. And for Maya and Quinn; may your lives be filled with monsters—the good kind.

—ZACK

I would like to thank my family, especially my Mom. Thank you so much for all of your support and encouragement. For teaching me to follow my dreams and never give up.

—ELEONORA

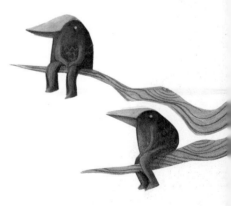

CONTENTS

Introduction
CONCERNING YOKAI

THE WORLD IS FULL OF MONSTERS. Big ones and small ones. Scaly ones and furry ones. Funny ones and scary ones. Some look like animals. Some are almost human. Some are anything but. Monsters come in every shape and size, limited only by our imagination. And they have always been with us. Every culture in every era creates their own monsters. These monsters go by many different names in many different languages. In Japan, they are called yokai.

Yokai are as much a part of Japan as sushi and samurai, as geisha and Godzilla. The Japanese have been telling yokai stories for thousands of years. There is no sign they will ever stop. In modern Japan, yokai are everywhere. You can see movies and cartoons about yokai. You can read books about yokai. There are hundreds of yokai video games. Yokai food like kitsune udon and tanuki soba are based on Japan's magical foxes and raccoon dogs. Yokai are in TV commercials and in comic books. They are on restaurant signs and clothing lines. Yokai are even on toilet paper (really!).

Yokai can be almost anything. They are piles of garbage come to life. They are devils from the darkest pits of hell. They are unnatural winds and old trees. Some, like the kappa, have complicated stories and deep mythology. Some, like the akashita, have no stories at all. They are just a line or two accompanying a picture. They can be native to Japan or imported from somewhere else. They can be ancient folklore or creations of modern pop culture. While every country loves their monsters, Japan seems to love them a little bit more. Japan is monster country.

In Japan, stories about yokai can be as random as the monsters themselves. Traditional tales are rarely complete stories, with a beginning, middle, or end. They don't teach lessons or morals. Most yokai stories are a recognition of wonder. They delight in the weird. They embrace shadows and the unexplainable parts of the world. And most importantly, yokai stories are often told as true stories. Japan has always embraced belief in yokai, even when common sense says not to.

The collection of yokai continually grows and changes. As old yokai are forgotten, new ones appear. And they travel. Yokai escaped their home country to become part of world culture. Games like Pokémon and Yo-kai Watch and movies like *Godzilla*, *Spirited Away*, and *My Neighbor Totoro* have made yokai familiar across the world. It's not unusual to see kappa pop up in American comics. Or for jorogumo spider women to appear on Western TV shows. The excellent weirdness of yokai transcends boundaries. Here's proof—Japan's yokai inspired a Swiss artist and an American writer to make this book.

In recognition of this international mix, our own *Yokai Stories* are set neverwhere and neverwhen. This isn't Japan, but isn't quite anywhere else. It's our own mish-mash world. Like the tales that inspired them, these yokai stories can be complete or just fragments. The stories invite readers to fill in the rest with their imagination. And like yokai themselves, the tales are a mix of new and old.

Although updated in language and setting, some are very old indeed. "The Dead Wife" comes from a twelfth-century book called *Konjaku monogatarishu* (*Tales of Times Now Past*). "Quinn and the Tanuki Dance" is adapted from the Edo-period story "The Procession of the Tanuki" which was known as one of the Seven Wonders of Honjo. The story "Shigeru and the

Kitsune Girl" is liberally adapted from "The Loving Fox," from the 1254 book *Kokonchomonju* (the title means "things seen and heard, old and new"; and confession time: I couldn't resist giving "The Loving Fox" a happy ending—in the original tale the poor fox girl dies). Some, like the lazy boy and the kappa in "Akira and the Three Kappa," are a blend of multiple stories with added twists. And some are new yokai stories entirely of our own invention. I leave it up to you to decide which is which.

All stories in this book share one thing. They are inspired by the brilliant art of Eleonora D'Onofrio. Eleonora and I met on the internet—a very modern way to share a love of things very old. When I saw her yokai art, I was taken with her unique style. Her paintings didn't seem bound to time or place. And the yokai in her art looked like they had something to say. Every picture seemed to be bursting with stories. To make this book, I took

Eleonara's art and did my best to find those stories. Instead of an illustrated story you could say these are storified illustrations. The art was the beginning, the story the end.

Together, this is our love letter to the wonderful world of yokai. It is also our own small part in adding a chapter or two to the never-ending book of yokai stories.

—ZACK DAVISSON

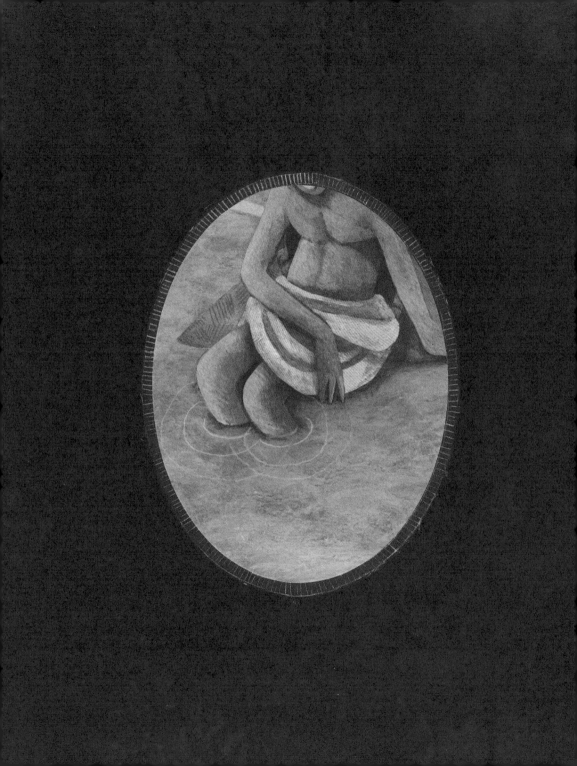

1

Akira & the THREE KAPPA

AKIRA NEVER WANTED TO DO ANYTHING. At least that's what his mother thought. And his father. And his brothers and sisters. And his teachers. And his…you get the idea. He never wanted to play sports. He never wanted to go camping, or to the beach, or to a friend's house. He never wanted to do his homework. If his family went to a baseball game or a picnic or a movie, he whimpered about not wanting to go. But Akira didn't see this as a problem. It wasn't that he hated all that stuff. He just loved to read.

When Akira came home from school, he dropped his coat on the floor, went straight to his room and grabbed a book off the shelf. He sank into books the way you might settle into a warm bath, soaking up ideas and facts and fantasies. When his mother told him he needed to get out more, to do things, Akira didn't see the point. Nothing out there was better than what was in a book.

What Akira dreaded most was warm summer days. No one cared what you did when it was pouring outside. No one yelled at you when it was dark and cold. But as soon as a yellow sun popped up in a blue sky, his mother would glare at him. Seeing her son, curled up on the sofa, nose wedged in a book, his mother would say the thing Akira hated most to hear:

"Akira, go do something. Go outside and play."

After a useless revolt, Akira would find himself kicked out the door, blinking in the sunshine. His mom would pack him a lunch and a bottle of water and tell him not to come home until sundown. Then, he would fall into the one thing he didn't mind doing outside—Akira liked to walk and read. Setting his feet on one of the many paths in the forest near his home, Akira would hold a book up to his face like a shield and just start walking. Today, like any other day, off he went. It must have been a particularly good book; there were dragons and gold and a collection of dwarves. Akira just kept walking and walking and walking not paying the slightest bit of attention to where he was going. He walked past trees and bushes and rocks. He walked past bugs and critters and mushrooms, all without noticing. He was so deep into his book that he didn't even see the thing lying across his path until he tripped over it. His book went flying while Akira tumbled into the dirt.

"What was that?" Akira said.

It was a body. Small and green; child-sized with scaly skin, like a turtle crossed with a monkey. Akira had read enough old folk stories to know a kappa when he stumbled upon one. His Grandma Nunoe had loved telling old tales. She had given him a collection of folklore books when he was young. Reading all his books had given Akira an open mind on monsters—after all, if there could be a monster in Loch Ness and a hairy bigfoot in the Pacific Northwest, why not a kappa in his forest? Stranger things did happen.

Although, this stranger thing was almost too strange. One thing Akira knew about kappa was that they shouldn't be away from the water. They had little bowls on their heads, and if that bowl dried out the kappa would die. This one looked pretty close; only a damp sheen glistened in a bowl that should have been full of water.

Akira thought he was lucky to find the kappa on dry land. He knew what kappa did to kids they caught swimming in the creek. They had a fondness for human liver, and weren't too fussy about how they got it. They stuck their hand in and yanked it out. Akira immediately sat down.

"A real kappa." Akira said. "Who would have thought?".

He grabbed a nearby stick and poked it. He first tapped it on its turtle shell. After a few raps, he got courageous enough to poke it in the soft bits. With the fifth poke, the kappa exhaled suddenly. Its breath smelling like the soft ground after a summer rain. A single eye slowly winked open from the scaled face. Its beak began to move.

"H-help me," the kappa whispered.

"Help you?" Akira skootched back, startled by the strange creature suddenly speaking to him. "No way! I know what kappa do!"

"Not that. Please, h-help me. I promise…anything. Nearby is a river. I have two brothers that live there. Each of them," he wheezed, "has a great treasure. Take me there…and I promise… you can have what you like. You can ch-choose. Please…"

Akira knew enough about magical creatures to know that with them, a promise is a promise. They may be evil and nasty and rip out your liver to eat, but they would never do anything as disgusting as break their word. So he took out his water bottle and poured some of the water into the kappa's bowl. The change in the creature was fantastic. It leapt straight up from the ground and did a fast-paced jig. Then it grabbed the bottle and poured all the water into its bowl. The kappa looked at Akira with inhuman eyes.

"And now for you…" the kappa smiled, its voice slightly menacing. It knew Akira was afraid.

"H-hey! You promised!" Akira jumped backwards.

"And a promise is a promise." The kappa smiled in its best attempt to look trustworthy. "Walk with me and we'll come to a bridge over a river. My two brothers are there. When we arrive, I'll swim out first and talk to them. They'll know not to harm you. Then you can have your pick of their treasures to take home. Whatever you wish."

Akira was wary, but followed behind the monster. The kappa skipped along at a steady pace. Sure enough, they came to a river. A bridge crossed over, exactly as the kappa had described. Seeing its home, the kappa was so happy that it sped up, running as fast as it could. It plunged straight into the water.

"Hey now! If you're lying and trying to get away…"

The kappa popped its head up from the water, looking back.

"Trust me," it said. "I'll be right back."

The boy soon saw something emerge from the water. Well, three somethings, including the kappa that Akira had rescued. However, where that kappa had been friendly and small, its two brothers were huge and menacing. Their skin was rough and deeply scaled, and their elbows and knees were bony and hooked. The oldest brother glared at Akira with menace in his eyes.

"We hear that you rescued our little brother, and that he made you a promise," the eldest brother croaked. "Well, a promise made is a promise kept. We have two treasures for you to choose from."

The biggest kappa reached into the water and produced a heavy wooden mallet. It looked old. Very old. And radiated power.

"This mallet is magic," the kappa said. "Take it and strike a stone. A single grain of rice will appear. If you shout the name of something before you strike the mallet, then that thing will appear. Gold. Diamonds. Horses. Even pizza. Your every wish is yours."

Akira looked at the mallet and knew the kappa was telling the truth. But then he thought back to some books he had read; it seems he heard a story once about a boy who got a magic hammer that gave him everything he wanted. It was great at first. His parents were overjoyed. But then, Akira remembered, the boy's parents became greedy. They took the hammer and used it to make themselves rich. Then neighbors heard of their fortune, and tried to kill the family and steal the hammer. Akira couldn't remember all the details of the story but he was sure everyone came to a very bad end. The magic mallet didn't bring any happiness at all. Just greed.

"Hmmm…I don't think so," Akira replied. "What else do you have?"

The second kappa, a little bit smaller but no less thorny and burly than his brother, reached into the water and produced an oyster. Gently wedging the oyster open, he pulled a small, hard case. The case looked like it was made of ebony, with a skeleton carved on the lid. From inside the case, he withdrew a tiny needle. It was like a little sewing needle, and glinted in the sunlight.

"This is the Resurrection Needle," the kappa said, its voice reedy and thin. "A great and powerful artifact. If you prick a dead person with this needle, they come back to life. You had a beloved grandmother once, didn't you? With just a little poke you can have her back, baking you cookies and reading you stories just like she used to."

This one made Akira's heart cry with longing. He did love his Grandma Nunoe and thought that there could be no greater treasure than having her back. But he remembered the stories she told him…like one about a boy who got a magic needle that could bring people back to life. It seemed amazing and wonderful at first, but as so often happens in these stories things turned out badly. The dead were not happy about being brought back. Living people heard about it and tried to take the needle from the boy. Wars were fought. Far more people died fighting for the needle than were brought back by it. Akira was pretty sure the boy committed suicide at the end. It was one of the most terrible stories. He didn't like to think about that one at all.

"No, I don't think so." Akira shuddered to himself.

"Well we must give you something!" said the kappa Akira had rescued.

Compared to his two brothers, this kappa was much less frightening. He almost looked friendly—if you can call such a monster friendly. He too reached into the water and brought up a little sack. He put his hand inside and pulled out something green.

"Here," it said, holding out a cucumber.

"What is that?"

"A cucumber."

Akira knew that kappa loved cucumbers. It was their favorite food. In fact, it was said that if you wanted to befriend local kappa, you had to write your name on a cucumber and drop it into a river. At least that was what the stories said. But still…

"Is it some sort of magic cucumber?" Akira asked. "Does it turn mud into gold, or grow a magic beanstalk? Can it be eaten forever without running out? Something like that?"

"Nope. Just a cucumber," it said. "I stole it from a farmer this morning. That's where I was going—to try and get some more. But I got lost on the path and wandered where you found me."

"No magic at all? No surprises?"

"Nothing. It is a particularly ordinary cucumber. But quite delicious. I ate two of its fellows today and they were scrumptious. That farmer knows what he is doing."

Akira thought and thought and wracked his brains, going through all of the stories he had ever heard. Sure, there were stories of magic vegetables and people coming to bad ends, or living happily ever after depending on where the story was written. But a plain, ordinary cucumber? Akira had to admit that he had never heard of a single bad thing that ever happened to a kid who ate their vegetables.

"OK," said Akira.

And with that, the third kappa swam over and handed Akira the cucumber. Akira was nervous to get that close to a kappa in water—the stories told him exactly what could happen—but the kappa did as he'd said, never once threatening Akira. The boy took the cucumber and had to admit that it did look very nice. Magic or not, it was a fine vegetable.

He was about to eat the cucumber, when he saw the sad look on the kappa's face. It couldn't quite frown, but the beaky mouth had a definite downcast look to it, a twist in the corners.

Akira understood that the kappa really didn't want to part with his treasure. But a promise was a promise. Feeling sorry for it, Akira snapped the cucumber in two and offered the kappa half.

"Here."

"Th-thank you," the kappa said, shocked at the offered delight. He reached for the cucumber shyly. Taking it from Akira, the kappa grinned as much as his beaky mouth allowed. Munching happily on the cucumber, he jumped back into the water. The kappa swam about halfway to the middle of the river, when he suddenly turned around and waved back at Akira.

"If you want to come and play with me some time, I won't mind," the kappa said, its beaked mouth almost smiling. "I won't kill you."

"I promise," it said, plunging in the water and swimming away to wherever kappa live.

Akira smiled too. Tracing back his path, he picked up his book from where it had been thrown, and went walking home, satisfied with how things had turned out. Munching on his cucumber, he had the oddest feeling. Somehow he knew that when he got home, he wouldn't read a book. It seemed like for the first time in his life, instead of reading about someone else's adventure, he had had his own. He laughed at the idea. His mom would be so proud; he finally did something. And instead of reading a book when he got home, this time, Akira thought to himself, maybe he would do something else—maybe he would write a book instead.

Mariko & the
AKASHITA

"MARIKO! YOU GET BACK HERE THIS INSTANT! You are *not* going to school like that this morning!"

Mariko had almost made it out the front door before being called back in. There was a brief moment when she thought about running down the street pretending not to hear, but she knew that would just make her mother come screaming after her, causing even more embarrassment in front of all her friends. No, better just to go back inside and see what the problem was. Mariko planted a right foot in front of her, pivoted around, and went back in the house. She dropped her backpack, and indulged herself in another deep sigh.

"What is it this time?" Mariko said. "Lunch? Got it. Rain?

Umbrella's right here, just in case."

"Oh no," said her mother, "much worse. The weather sorcerer said an akashita was spotted over Mr. McGregor's fields this morning. A big one, floating in the clouds."

"But that's miles away! And I'll be to school before anything could happen!" Mariko stomped her foot in defiance. "It's not like—"

"You can take that chance when you're older, but while you live here I think for you," her mother said. "You know what the akashita means! Don't you remember what happened to Ms. Miura two years ago? Walked right under the akashita without a care in the world, and then—*wham!*—hit by a train a few days later.

"Now put on your white vest with the protection charms— I know you think it looks stupid, but better to look like a fool than to act like one." Mariko's mother was already slipping the vest over her.

"Fine." Mariko sighed sullenly.

It was so lame. A white cotton vest, covered with magical symbols. Her mother was always like this. Weather sorcerers. Fortune tellers. Feng shui. (Mariko's bed had to be turned a certain direction to help with her studies.) They planted herbs in the garden to "ward off evil." What century was this? At least she wouldn't be the only one wearing the stupid thing. Other people at school had superstitious moms. But not all of them; and they would laugh at her.

She had no choice except to put on the vest—but that didn't mean she had to like it. Mariko tried to plead her case. "I still don't get it. It doesn't make any sense." Mariko said. "A giant red monster floating in the clouds, with a big red tongue, and if you see it you get back luck. What is that? Where does this thing live? How does it give you bad luck? Why? At least with things like Santa Claus you get details."

Mariko pushed on, "The akashita's not even a good story! Like that boy who met the oni and tricked him into stealing his zits. Or that one you read me in the newspaper about the boy from the next town over who wrote about meeting kappa! At least those made some kind of sense. This akashita is just… weird."

"Listen." Mariko's mom said, "The world doesn't always make sense. Sometimes things are mysterious, and you can't understand them. You just accept them. You allow yourself to be amazed, and maybe a little scared, but you don't try to look for answers. It's like the old saying, 'from an open mouth flows a river of troubles.' Sometimes you just shut your mouth and don't ask any questions. That's life."

"Not my life," replied Mariko defiantly. "Maybe you don't mind not knowing all this stuff, but I'll never stop asking questions!"

"Well then," said her mother, with a hint of a smile, surveying her charge safe in her white vest. She spoke in a voice that only a mother can use for their own child, speaking with absolute certainty that what she was about to say was going to happen:

"You shall have to become a scientist."

No. 3

Maya & the BAKU

WAS IT A LOUD SCREAM? It sounded like a loud scream. With dream screams Maya was never sure, because while they sounded loud in her head that didn't mean anyone else could hear them. Since mom and dad didn't come running into her room to see what was wrong, Maya had to assume this was just a dream scream—she hadn't made any noise out loud. But that didn't make the dream any less scary. Maya had lots of scary dreams. She didn't like them at all.

She winced one eye open and wasn't entirely sure that she wasn't still dreaming. After all, there was clearly a monster at the foot of her bed. It looked weird, like a whole bunch of parts put together in the wrong order. An elephant nose on a hairy pig's

body; it looked like something she'd seen a zoo once, but not quite. A tapir. That was it. It looked like a dream version of a tapir, or maybe it didn't look like that at all. Whatever it was, its strangest trait wasn't its long nose or its human eyes that were clearly watching her. The strangest thing was that it wasn't frightening in the least bit.

"I'm not scared of you. Why am I not scared of you?" Maya whispered.

"Because I don't wish you to be scared of me," the creature replied. Its voice was gentle and soothing, yet not entirely human. It sounded like a memory...

"I am a baku—a dream eater. I come from a land both far away and very near, a land that you visit every night. I heard you call to me, and so I came. I'm not the king of my realm, but I offer a special service to some. If you want, if you ask me to, I can take away your dreams. Eat them all up and swallow them so that they never trouble you again."

"All of my dreams?" Maya asked. "All of the bad dreams that I have every night? That're so scary that I'm afraid to go to sleep? I'd never have to see them again?"

"All of them," it said. "Your sleep would be blissful peace to the end of your days. Each night you would close your eyes and each morning you would open them again, and in between would be nothing. Absolutely nothing. Without dreams, you would never visit my land again."

"But they aren't ALL bad dreams," Maya said. "I have good dreams too—like dreams of things that could never happen, like being a princess on a pirate ship, or even normal things like playing with my friends. Or dreams of things that might happen, like going to Rome or being an astronaut. Would I have to lose all those dreams too? Can't you just take the bad ones?"

"Dreams are dreams," replied the baku. "Who can tell if they are good or bad? A dream that scares you now might inspire you in the future. A long-cherished dream today becomes the childish fantasy of tomorrow. I am a baku—a dream eater. I cannot sort between good dreams or bad, or tell you which ones you should listen to and which ones you should forget. I can do only one thing. I can eat them all away."

"My dreams are so scary," Maya said, her voice trembling, drawing herself up into her covers, "every time I close my eyes, it's like the monsters come. And the more scared I am, the scarier my dreams are. But I don't want to have no dreams at all. Sometimes nice things happen in my dreams. Sometimes I see my dog Logan, who isn't here anymore. Sometimes I see my brother Quinn and my dad and mom. But that's not all the time. Most of the time I'm so scared I wake myself up screaming. What else can I do?"

"You can be brave." The baku whispered.

His eyes looking at her with a compassion and love that the young girl had never seen before. She knew at that moment that he was something far, far beyond human. Not quite a god, but something near. It gave her courage.

"I think," Maya said, rolling her thoughts over in her head, knowing that once she made her choice it would be made forever, and there would be no taking it back, "I think that nothing could be worse than a life without any dreams at all. So thank you, Mr. Baku. But you will have to go hungry tonight."

"So be it," said the baku, slipping back into the shadows and disappearing from her room. And while Maya could not say for sure, she remembered her entire life the look on the baku's face as it faded away—it almost looked like it was smiling.

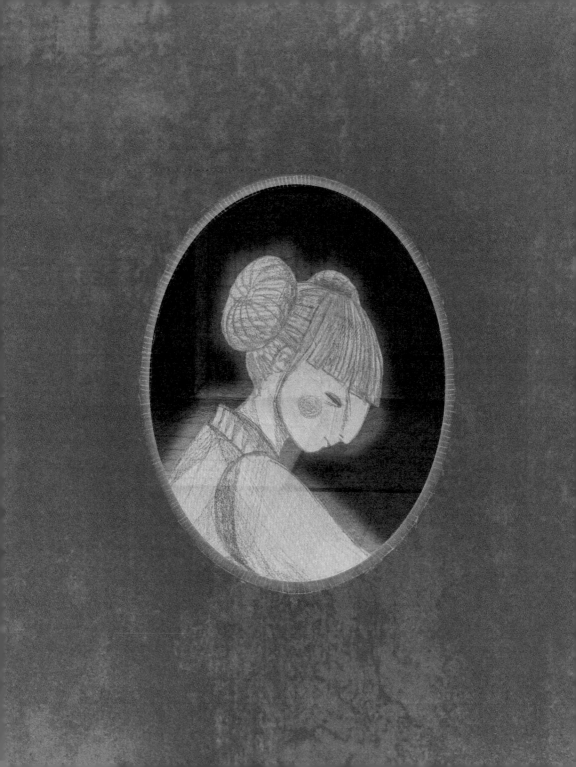

Miyuki's
NEW JOB

"SCRUB THE FLOOR." Miyuki thought, "Scrub the floor. Back and forth, scrub the floor. That's what I'll do all day, just as boring as at home." When Miyuki's mom had gotten her this job for the summer, she had thought it would be exciting…not this. She at least had been hoping to make a friend.

After all, the Kashiba Inn was famous. It was almost three hundred years old, very expensive and very high class. Rich people stayed there. Sometimes even celebrities. And that was before they did that TV documentary. Now, people came from all over the world to stay at the haunted hotel. Miyuki wasn't put off by that—she knew a thing or two about ghosts. Besides, that meant even more interesting people would be coming.

Who knew what might happen?

And then she saw where she was going to work.

Miyuki couldn't have been more disappointed. Instead of fabulous spaces filled with fancy people, the mistress of the inn led her to a small, ancient room far off to the side of the regular hotel. "Your job is to clean this room," the mistress said.

The room looked much older than the rest of the building. Miyuki thought it must have been here first and that the hotel was built around it. It was dark inside, and poorly lit by old paper windows.

"That's all you have to do." The mistress said. "You don't go anywhere else. You don't look at anyone else. You don't speak to anyone. You have one job—make sure that not a speck of dust settles in this room."

Miyuki had seen the mistress on television. She was just as glamorous and intimidating as expected. She dressed in an expensive kimono with a real fur collar. It was impossible to tell how old she was. Miyuki was scared of her, but still managed to squeak out: "Why?"

"Am I paying you to ask questions?" The mistress let out an exaggerated sigh. "Your mother said you were a hard worker, and she swore you had some special talent that made you a good fit for the job—whatever that means. But she didn't say you were nosy! Okay, listen closely, and I'll tell you a secret."

The mistress leaned in close, lowering her voice to a conspiratorial whisper. "Everyone knows this hotel is haunted. It's on the website. We sell those protection amulets and junk in the gift shop. I don't think most people believe it's real, but it gives them a thrill to stay here and as long as they keep paying that's good enough for me.

"So here's the secret," she said, the corners of her mouth turning up into a sly smile. "The ghost is real. And this is where it…lives, if you can say that about a dead person.

"Now," the mistress leaned back, returning to her usual sharp self, "you know there are different kinds of ghost. You've heard of the zashiki warashi, the little house ghost that blesses a place with good fortune, right?"

"Of course." Miyuki smirked back. Everyone knew what that was.

"Well there is another kind of zashiki warashi—an even better kind!" the mistress said. "This little ghost is called a chopirako. Have you heard of that?"

"Nooo," Miyuki said.

"Well! That shows you didn't read our website after all! Our chopirako is part of the advertising." It was the mistress's turn to smirk.

"Anyways," she continued, "a chopirako is a delicate spirit. Maybe some lord's pampered kid who died ages ago? Who knows? All I know is, they say if you keep her happy and her room spotless, she'll bless you with good fortune.

"I don't know if I believe it," the mistress said as she reached into a cupboard and started bringing out cleaning supplies. She set them next to a bucket of soapy water that was already there. "I've never seen anything myself, nor has anyone else so far as I know. The one thing I know is, the room is always messy. It gets cleaned every day, and it's dirty the next day. There are all these spots that appear, like something's been knocking about. Maybe it's mold from the ceiling. I don't pretend to know.

"What I do know," the mistress said, "is that real or not, you don't mess with a good thing. When I bought this place, the legend came with it. If the success of this inn depends on keeping some ghost girl happy, then so be it! Now," the mistress shoved Miyuki into the little room. She set the bucket down carefully, and then tossed the cleaning supplies and scrub brush in after. "Get to work."

And that was it. Miyuki looked around the little room, and saw her dreams of an action-packed summer crushed. She sighed deeply and picked up the brush and put it in the soapy water. "I guess I better get started," Miyuki said out loud. "Scrub the floor, back and forth, scrub the floor."

After about thirty minutes of this, Miyuki's mind began to wander. Was there really a dead girl here? It was possible. And Miyuki's mother was right about one thing. She did have a special talent that made her a good fit for this job, even though it wasn't something she was really proud of. Normally she tried to hide it. But now...well, she might as well find out.

"Hey ghost girl!" Miyuki shouted, "Are you in here?"

The room was silent.

Miyuki waited, listening closely. She put down her scrub brush and tried to relax her senses, to really open herself to the room. She swore she could almost hear the faint bouncing of a ball.

"Come on!" Miyuki shouted again. "It looks like I'm going to be stuck in this room all summer, so you might as well come out!"

The bouncing ball sound became clear. A hesitant voice drifted from a gloomy back corner.

"Can...can you...talk to me?" the voice said. "See me?"

Looking closely, Miyuki saw a young girl. She slowly appeared, like a picture coming into focus. Dressed in clothes like something out of an old movie, the girl was kneeling on the tatami mats and bouncing a little ball.

"No one can ever see me, but you can see me!" said the ghost girl. "I've been alone a long time. And lonely. No one to play with."

Miyuki's eyes grew wide, and she wasn't sure what to say. Miyuki had always been able to see things other people couldn't—reikan, her mother called it. But usually it was just flashes and sensations. It was a shock to be face to face with an actual ghost. An actual chopirako.

"You're...wow." Miyuki stammered. "Wha...what's your name?"

"My name's Ohara." The little ghost girl did a formal bow. "I have haunted this place for three hundred years. Th-this was my room. I suppose it still is."

"I'm Miyuki," she said. "And I'm...the maid, I guess. I'm here to clean your room. And keep you happy, I think."

"Oh," Ohara said, a bit sadly. "Is that all? You know, for three hundred years now I've had to watch people cleaning my room. First my parents, and then whoever bought the house after them, and then maids when the inn was built. At first I liked it. It made me feel special and important. But now I'm bored. For the past century I've been making a mess on purpose just to see if anyone will notice.

"Hey Miyuki," Ohara said mischievously, "I have an idea. Instead of scrubbing the floors with that stupid brush back and forth like everyone else has done...why don't you play with me instead?"

"Besides…" Ohana carefully aimed her ball, and tossed it with enough strength to tip the soapy water bucket, sending it sprawling. She laughed delightedly. "I like things a little messy."

Miyuki couldn't help laughing in return. She went to grab the ball. It looked like this was going to be a fun summer after all. And she just might make a friend.

The Cave of the
JOROGUMO

"COME IN, BOY. Come in and have a good look. It's what you came for, after all. And I would hate for you to have come all this way and not get what you came for."

The woman lounged in her chair, a kimono of silk draped across her shoulder. She was beautiful—no, not beautiful. That basic, simple word did not fit her at all. Chiaki didn't know exactly what word to use. For the first time in his life he wished he had studied more in school, learned something fancier so that he would be able to describe what was right before his eyes. But it was too late. There he was. And there she was. Looking into her eyes, Chiaki knew he had made the greatest mistake of his life.

It seemed a long time ago that Chiaki had stood at the foot

of this mountain, looking up at a waterfall high up on the slope. They were on a high school field trip and his friends Akira and Mariko were talking about it. No—that was a lie. They weren't his friends. Akira the bookworm and Mariko his nerd girlfriend— they met last year in junior high school and had been together ever since. They were a happy couple, so naturally Chiaki made them his target. He was a bully. He knew it. Chiaki was never good at much, but he was good at that. Besides, there was a natural order to these things. Spiders ate flies. And this whole mess was that geek's fault anyways.

"See up there?" Akira said. "That's Joren Falls. Behind that is the cave of the Jorogumo—the spider woman. I read about it in an old book. It said she's the most beautiful woman on earth, but if she catches you she'll wrap you up and eat you alive."

"Niiiice." Mariko said.

Up in the cave, Chiaki struggled to hold on. He was terrified, but could not run away.

"Come in," the woman whispered to Chiaki sweetly. Her voice was like silk. So soft. So fine. It seemed to pour out from her mouth, wrapping around him like a cocoon, drawing him in. Chiaki moved further into his cave, against his will. The cave was dark and hard to see; but he could see her. She almost glowed. And her eyes—too many of them—her eyes drew him towards her.

As he walked, he felt something crunching under his feet.

"Are you sure you should be talking to me about 'the most beautiful woman on earth?'" Mariko smiled sweetly, but with a hint of warning. "Maybe you want to sit by yourself on the bus ride back!"

"Maybe you want to sit by me, Mariko," Chiaki said as he wedged himself between them, ignoring the looks on their faces. "So you're saying there's some hot chick up there? Think she's lonely after all these years and needs a little company?"

"As if you are brave enough to go." Akira snickered. Mariko busted out laughing. And that was that. Chiaki wasn't going to be called a coward. A dare was delivered. A dare accepted. And that night Chiaki found himself sneaking out to climb up the mountain. There was nothing to be scared of. He didn't expect to find anything. He never thought he would...

Against his will, his feet carried him further into the cave.

"Bones, boy." She smiled. "Five hundred years' worth of bones. Five hundred years' worth of brave idiots with more guts than brains. Men. Women. Adults. Children. All of them had one thing in common—they couldn't resist my lure. They climbed here to test their courage. To face the spider woman. And here they stayed. Just like you."

Chiaki's mind was in a daze. Trying to put thoughts together

was like swimming in honey. All he could hear was her voice. All he could see was her eyes. As he walked slowly over a carpet of bones, getting ever closer to the woman, he knew there was something he should remember—something he should say. What was it? Something Akira said. Something…from a book…

"She's super evil. There's a way out though," Akira said. "The book says you have to promise to never tell. If you do that, she lets you go free."

"That's stupid, Akira," Mariko replied. "How scary can a monster be who lets you go just because you ask nicely? Isn't that the same legend as the snow lady? Old fairytale writers just ripped each other off. Your stories are way better."

"I p…p…promise." Chiaki managed to get the words out of his mouth. It might have been the hardest thing he had ever done in his life. Each syllable was a struggle.

"I p…promise not to…t…tell." Chiaki summoned his willpower. "If…you let me go. I promise not to tell. Anyone. Ever. I promise."

The Jorogumo tittered with delight. Her laugh was magic, like tinkling bells.

"The book! You read the book! Oh, you dear, sweet, delightful boy! You really have made my night, you know. To think that after so many centuries that book is still doing its work… Ha ha ha! And did you really think I would let you go just because you asked nicely? Because you promised? It really is too wonderful."

She finally stood up from her seat. Chiaki froze in fear as he saw eight legs extend behind her. The sweetness of her spell disappeared, and he was now held by absolute terror. Her spider's body unfurled, stretching like a cat after a long nap. She rose in height until she towered over the boy. Moving in closely, she reached out a hand to stroke Chiaki's cheek.

"I could let you go, I suppose," she said. "You know, since you promised so earnestly. But alas, a girl does get hungry. Meals don't come as often as they used to. And besides…"

Her face drew closer to Chiaki as she whispered into his ear. "Who do you think wrote that book in the first place?"

 No. 6

Conversation with a
KEUKEGEN

YEP. IT'S ME. KEUKEGEN—the dirt monster. Oh, I know, I look like a fluffy dog.
Maybe you're thinking you want to pet
me? I won't say no—I wouldn't mind a
little affection—but you might not like
what your hand looks like after. You see,
that's not fur. No, siree. That's all the dirt
and grime and filth from all the corners
of your house that you never clean. Well,
there is some fur—the dog hair under
the couch. There's also food droppings
from under the oven. And what the cat

did waaaay back in the closet that you smelled for weeks but never found. Let it all lie around for long enough and poof! It comes to life! That's me…like a magical Frosty the Snowman! But instead of beloved by children and made of Christmas snow, I'm made out of the yuckiest stuff around and hated by pretty much everyone.

What can a monster do? Not all yokai are created equal, I guess. Sure, some get to be mysterious dream eaters, some get to be spooky spider ladies, and heck, some even get to be disembodied heads on flaming wagon wheels! How cool would that be? And then some of us get to be animated trash heaps. That's life. You get what you get.

I'm going to be honest—I wasn't always so relaxed about this. There was a time when I was really upset. Angry, even. After all, if you want to be the least popular yokai around, try being a living garbage pile. I tried being cool, but let's face it, that wasn't going to work. Then I got really angry and tried being a bad guy. I'd thought I'd get back at everyone. I hung around and made people sick—but that only made me lonelier.

It sucks. I wish I was something else, but I'm not. We don't get to choose.

Can't complain though. Better than being nothing, right? I lurk around in the shadows. Sometimes I watch the TV when you got it on. I kinda wish you had better taste but I don't get to pick my humans. Oh hey, you know when you leave the house, and you come back and the remote control is under the couch? Guilty! That is me. Sorry!

Anyways, I'll slink back into the shadows now. Just wanted to pop my stinky paws out and say hi. And maybe ask you a favor. Next time you eat, don't be so careful about cleaning up. If some food falls, just kick it under the stove. Same with those cupboards. No need to haul everything out and dust them. They're fine. And no need to vacuum under the furniture, right? Just let that filth stay where it is. Maybe it will come to life! You see, to tell the truth… I'm a little lonely.

I could use a friend…

Shigeru & the
KITSUNE GIRL

THIS STORY COMES FROM A LONG TIME AGO. Not *terribly* long ago; maybe your grandparents' time, or your great-grandparents' depending on how old you are when you read this. In any case, long enough ago that things were different.

A young boy named Shigeru was wandering the riverbank. His family's house was up near the mountains. There weren't many people around. Almost no kids his own age, and the ones that were there didn't like Shigeru. But that was OK. Shigeru liked being alone. He was what they called an "odd boy." He lived more in his imagination than in the real world. The one thing Shigeru hated was being cooped up. He'd much rather be in fresh air with the promise of adventure.

Today he was outside, enjoying the crisp autumn weather and bright colors. He wasn't doing much, kicking fallen leaves and being happy at the crunchy sounds they made. Every now and then he would pick up a stick for an imaginary sword fight. He thrust and riposted, defending himself from all manner of shrubbery. Needless to say, when he turned the corner of the river, Shigeru was entirely surprised to find a young girl crying.

It was odd enough for Shigeru to see another person in the woods, much less an unfamiliar girl. And what's more, Shigeru had never seen anyone so beautiful. Sitting on the river bank in her kimono, she looked like a picture. She was so sad. His heart broke as he saw her. He wanted to help, but didn't know what to do. At twelve years old, he didn't have much experience comforting crying people. Still, Shigeru did his best.

"Are…are you OK?" he managed to ask.

"Do I look like I'm OK?" the girl snapped back, "Is crying on a muddy riverbank your idea of OK? Yes," she said, her voice dripping with sarcasm. "I'm perfectly fine. Now go away and leave me alone."

Shigeru's words came pouring out.

"I'm s…sorry. I just wanted to help. My name's Shigeru. I was just going for a walk." The poor boy had no practice in talking to people, and it showed. "I like walking. It's nice, don't you think?

This is a good forest. Lots of trees." Shigeru was really trying hard now. "I found a really cool stick that I might take home. Are you from around here? I don't have many friends. To tell the truth," he brought his voice down to a whisper, "no one really likes me. I don't know why. I think I'm nice. My mom says that's just how people are.

"Hey!" Shigeru perked up, remembering something important. "Are you hungry? I got lunch."

Shigeru sat down next to the girl. Despite yelling at him earlier, she didn't seem to mind. He dug into his backpack and pulled out his lunch. A couple of rice balls. He offered one to the girl, and she accepted. They were good; his mom had made them.

"So why are you crying?" Shigeru asked.

"People don't like you? They hate me," the girl said bitterly. "I don't know why. It isn't anything I did. It's just who I am. They look at me, and they don't just say mean things to me." This time the girl's voice dropped to a whisper. "When they find out what I am—sometimes they even want to kill me."

"What are you talking about?" Shigeru said. "I don't see anything different about you. You look like a normal girl to me. Maybe prettier than other girls…" Shigeru blushed as he said out loud what he was thinking. The girl appeared not to notice.

"Look," the girl said, "I know you mean well, but you can't understand. Inside your little town you think everything's fine, and it is for you. But there are other towns, other places.

"The world is bigger than you know." She said, casting her head down. "And that's not something everyone likes. People like things small. Their imagination is small, so they want to keep the world small too. And when someone like me who comes along, and doesn't look like them, or act like them...all of the sudden they have to admit that this bigger world exists.

"And they don't like it." She said at last, closing her eyes to a painful memory. "So the easiest thing to do is erase the evidence. Erase me. Pretend people like me don't exist."

The girl leaned forward even further. As her tears fell they spread out in little circles, hiding her reflection. "I could just run away and hide," she said, "but I don't want to always be on the outside either. I want to come in. So that's why I'm crying...it sucks. I hate it. But it isn't going to change."

Shigeru shifted uneasily. He was trying to figure out what to say. He knew there was more going on here than he could really understand. Nothing in his life experience had prepared him for this moment. But somehow he felt a bond with this girl he had just met. It was a mysterious feeling—if he had to put a word to it he would call it fate. Or magic.

"I...I don't know what to say." Shigeru said, "I'm sorry people are mean to you. I don't want them to be. And you're right that I don't know much about the world, but that doesn't mean I don't want to. I mean, I know people aren't nice, especially to anyone who's different." Shigeru turned to look at her, and she turned to see him too. "Anyways," he said, "I don't hate you. For whatever that's worth. And I don't see what anyone has to hate about you anyways. You look…normal."

The girl looked him deep in his eyes. Shigeru somehow knew she was reading his soul. He couldn't think of anything else to do, so he decided to let her. He didn't hide anything. He opened to her completely. They stared at each other for a long time. Finally, she spoke.

"I don't always look like this," she whispered. "I can look normal for a little while. I can be a cute girl. But not all the time. And then someone finds out—someone always finds out, and it starts all over again."

"So what do you look like?" Shigeru said.

"I could…I could show you," she said, hesitantly. "But there's a catch. It's complicated. There are rules with my kind. Things that don't always make sense. It's like there's a curtain over the world, and once I lift it, it can never be closed again." She looked at him earnestly, "You would always see that bigger world. You'd never get to pretend again that you lived somewhere safe and small. You'd know…"

"That doesn't sound so bad," Shigeru said, although inside he was shaking. He thought about how your whole life can change in a single day, in a single meeting.

"There's one more thing… It's, well, it's kind of embarrassing, but…" Her face flushed red. "You'd have to marry me."

"WHAT!?!" Shigeru sputtered. "But I'm only…we just…"

"Not today. Not tomorrow. In fact, you won't even remember." She stared at her reflection again, unable to look Shigeru in the face. "If I show you, we'll part, and you'll forget, like a dream. But one day we'll meet again. And on that day you'll have to marry me. If you don't, I'll die. Like I said, it's complicated with my kind. Lots of rules.

"But," She said, "you have to choose. That's also one of the rules."

"Wow. Jeez." Shigeru looked away. "That's…I don't know…"

Shigeru felt like he was going to throw up. It seemed like his whole life was being decided in this one moment. And in fact it was. But was that a bad thing? Or was this his one chance— something that he needed to grab and hold on to? I guess he would never know for sure. But suddenly, he did know one thing, one thing. One thing absolutely for sure. He knew what his answer was.

"OK." Shigeru whispered.

"Are you sure?" She said.

"Yeah."

"Last chance."

"I'm sure."

The girl leaned over the river. The waters grew eerily still, like a mirror. Shigeru knew it wasn't natural. Maybe nothing in his life ever would be natural again. He was scared, more scared than he had ever been. But that didn't stop him from looking. He saw her.

Shigeru saw her true face in the water, the face of a fox. He saw all the magic she held, all the danger. He saw that she was one thing, and also another. She was…complicated. And Shigeru knew that to love her would also be…complicated. But that was OK.

Seeing her as she truly was, Shigeru said, "I think you're beautiful."

The girl sighed next to him, her whole body relaxing at once. Shigeru realized she was just as scared as he was. Still looking at her reflection in the water, he reached over to hold her hand.

"What's your name?" Shigeru asked, his voice quavering.

"My name is Nunoe," she answered, her voice matching Shigeru's own.

"That's a nice name," Shigeru said.

"Thanks." She smiled.

"I'm Shigeru."

DECADES LATER, Shigeru still liked holding Nunoe's hand, now wrinkled and weathered with age. But beautiful. Always beautiful. As they sat in their own home, watching the fire, she glanced over to him and saw him deep in thought.

"What are you thinking?" She said.

"Of the day we first met," he answered.

Nunoe smiled. She got up to make some tea, while Shigeru started to tidy up. Their grandson Akira would be coming over soon. There was something odd about that boy, Shigeru thought. Maybe he took after his grandmother.

"Do you ever regret your answer?" she said, bringing him some tea. "I gave you a choice, you know. This is all your fault!"

She smacked him with a couch cushion, making him laugh. But then he got very serious.

"Never." Shigeru answered seriously. "Not for a single moment."

The Lure of the
NURE ONNA

"HOLD MY BABY."

"No."

"Please? Just for a second. I gotta do this thing real quick, and if you would hold my baby that would be a big help."

"No."

"Why not?"

"You're a giant snake lady."

"I'm not!"

"You are. You're not even trying. I can see your snake tail and everything, just under the water. What's your game? You ask some nice guy to hold your baby—that probably isn't even a real baby—and then when I'm helpless you attack and kill me?

No thanks. I wasn't born yesterday."

"Oh, so that's how it is, is it? You think just because I'm a giant snake woman that I can't be nice? Maybe you shouldn't judge people so much on their appearance? Maybe you should give a girl a chance before deciding she's an evil killer? Do you have any idea how hard it is for someone like me? Fine. You got me. I'm a giant snake lady. But that doesn't make me a bad person. Take a chance. After all, if I was trying to fool you I would have done more to hide my tail. Changed my appearance entirely. At least tried to cover up. But here I am, tail and all. Come on, please? Just for a second. Hold my baby? Please!?"

"Fine. You're right. I shouldn't judge people on appearances. That was wrong of me. Here, give me your baby. Huh, heavier than it looks…big guy, eh? Uhhh…wait, this isn't a baby! It's just a big rock wrapped in a blanket… Hey now…what are you…? You said… No! Stay back…"

"Sucker."

"Aaaaiiiiieeeeee!!!!!!"

The Smile of the OHAGURO BETTARI

FIVE GUYS WERE COMING HOME AFTER A NIGHT OUT. They'd been out having fun—maybe too much fun. Food was eaten. Drinks were drunk. Eventually the bars closed and it was time to go. Wanting to keep the party going, the five guys decided to walk home together. After all, it was a warm summer night.

Talking loudly and singing, they caroused through the quiet neighborhood. The guys' manners were poor at the best of times, but tonight was the worst. As they passed by the houses of people trying to sleep, more than a few windows slammed shut. More than a few people yelled at them. But they didn't care.

"Hey look!" one of them said, noticing something in the streetlights.

Up ahead, they saw the dark silhouettes of another group taking advantage of the warm summer night. A group of five girls were walking together, backs turned to the five boys. Unlike the obnoxious fivesome, these girls walked in absolute silence. Only the clack of their sandals on the pavement could be heard. They were dressed in a way that could be described as old-fashioned. Their sandals were made of wood. *Click, clack.*

"What do you say, fellows?" the same guy said, smirking. "Shall we get their attention?"

Without waiting for an answer from his friends, he shouted at the group of girls.

"Hey ladies! Nice night for a walk, huh?"

Another guy joined in. "You want some company? Looks like we got a matched set of numbers here! Whatta ya say?"

The five girls acted as if they had not even heard the shouted greeting. They kept walking forward at their slow, steady pace. *Click, clack.*

"Come on!" another guy shouted, annoyed at being ignored. "We're just trying to be friendly! The least you could do is talk to us! Don't be stuck up!"

At that, the ladies stopped dead in their tracks. Their wooden sandals ceased to clack on the pavement. They stood still for a moment. Then, in a single movement, they turned around. In the dark of the night, it was difficult to see their faces. Shadows covered everything but their mouths, which were shut tight like blank masks, with no expressions at all.

"That's better! See, we can all be friendly!" The guys moved in closer, thinking the girls were warming up to their charms. "Now why the sad faces? Pretty girls like you ought to smile! How about it? Can you give us a smile? Smile!"

In a single movement, the girls' mouths moved. In a single movement, the girls smiled…

The guys screamed.

The
DEAD WIFE

IT WAS A MELANCHOLY STORY. William and Naoko had seemed like the perfect couple. From the day they met they were always together, and no one at all was surprised when they got married. No, the surprise came later. After two years full of love and happiness, Naoko was struck by a suddenly illness. Sadly, she died.

William was beside himself. Like any normal person, he cried and cried at first, but then he continued to cry. He did nothing but mourn his lost wife, only doing the bare minimum to survive. It was like William had died too, only his body was still alive. His friends tried to comfort him and cheer him up. They did everything they could to get William back into the world and get him interested in life again. They invited him to parties. They tried to

set him up on dates. But nothing worked. Three years passed in this way. For three years William cried every day.

One summer night when William lay crying at home, he thought he heard something coming from the closed bedroom. He stopped crying and turned his ear to listen closely. He heard a voice saying "Please open this door and let me in." There was no mistake. It was Naoko.

William opened the door a crack, peeked into the room. He saw his dead wife standing there. She looked exactly as she had when she was still alive.

Seeing her, William was chilled to the bone and overcome with fear. His eyes went wide and his mouth hung open. He couldn't speak. Couldn't move. Finally, he screamed.

"So that's it?" Naoko said, disappointed. "You've been so sad weeping and longing for me for three years—three years!—that I couldn't get any kind of rest. Finally I come back to see you, and you can't even say hello? You just sit there shivering like a scared kid? You know what, if that's the kind of greeting I get, then I'm just going back!"

With that said, Naoko disappeared.

Mohan & the ONI

PIMPLES. ZITS. Acne. Blackheads. Spots. Call them what you will, Mohan had them. He was, without a doubt, the zittiest guy in sixth grade. And there wasn't anything he could do about it. He had tried creams. He had tried ointments. He swiped his face with pads. He stayed away from greasy foods. His mother took him to the doctor. Nothing. Finally, he gave up. In despair, he realized that he would have a face that looked like a painful red constellation for his whole life. And odds were good that life was going to suck.

In particular a girl named Jessica liked to make fun of him. Jessica had problems with zits herself, but she thought the best way to deal with it was to get everyone looking at Mohan.

She figured the more people were looking at him, the less they would notice her own zits. It had been working so far. Mohan was an easy target.

But he couldn't just sit around and feel bad all the time. Zits or not, Mohan had things to do. Everyone in the family worked, and his job was to hunt mushrooms. His family lived far away from town in the hills, amongst the woods where wild matsutake mushrooms grew. The mushrooms were expensive and selling them helped the family earn a living.

So on weekends, Mohan pulled on his boots, grabbed his bucket, and headed into the woods to see what he could find. He actually liked that part: going out into the forest alone, wandering among the trees and shrubs and animals. It was peaceful.

Except when it rained. The sky had been blue when he left the house, but after a few hours of hunting the weather changed. It started as a few drops spattering on his face, but then the rain came stronger and stronger. Mohan had never seen such rain—it felt like someone was trying to dump the entire ocean on him. He knew he was too far to make a run for home without being soaked, so he looked around for a place to stay dry. Fortunately rain this strong couldn't last very long. The storm would soon wear itself out. Looking around desperately, Mohan found a hollow tree that he could squeeze himself into. And so he did.

But the storm didn't end. Mohan stayed in that tree for what seemed like hours. Unlike a normal mountain shower, the rain gained in strength until the sky was alive with lightning and the earth shook with thunder. Mohan was terrified that the storm was going to rip apart his tree and him with it. But then suddenly it stopped, like a snap of the fingers. There was nothing natural about that either. Or what happened next.

"Ho ho ho! Pass me that pie! I'm hungry enough to eat a horse!"

Mohan heard voices. It sounded like someone was having a picnic—several someones, from what he could hear. They were calling for drink and food and being none too polite about it. All the voices were gruff and deep, but from his hiding spot he could make out seven distinct voices. Mohan was curious. He had to see what faces those voices were attached to.

Poking his head out of the hollow of the tree, he saw monsters. Big, scary monsters, as big as giants. They were bright red and dressed in tiger skins. Their heads were covered in horns, and their mouths were wide open. Mohan knew instantly that they were oni—fierce demons of the netherworld. Although he had never heard that they liked picnics.

Three of the oni were sitting around a fire, roasting meat and preparing food. Another three were singing and dancing, stomping their feet and bellowing loudly in a sort of wild hoedown. They looked like they were having a jolly time. A fourth, who looked like a boss, was sitting in a chair, watching the show. He scowled.

"Bah! The same dance again?" the boss oni said. "Don't you ever learn anything new? A jitterbug or a Charleston? Some hip-hop? Even the boot-scootin' boogie! Anything other than the same stomping I've seen for the last hundred years! I'll tear my eyes out!"

Now, aside from his acne troubles and his mushroom-gathering, there was something else interesting about Mohan. He loved to dance. He'd never taken a class, and didn't know any proper steps. Most of it he made up himself, doing little shimmies and leaps and moves, dancing around the forest when he thought he was all alone. So he was fascinated at watching these oni dance, even though he agreed with their boss—they sucked.

"Can't someone do better than this?" said the boss oni. "Anyone?"

Well now, that was a challenge that Mohan just couldn't resist. He knew that what he was about to do was dangerous—dancing for monsters seemed like a good way to get yourself killed. What if they didn't like his dance? Well, that was a chance he was willing to take... Mohan left the safety of his hollow tree and stepped into the light of the fire.

"You want to see some dancing?" Mohan said. "I can do better than that!"

Without waiting for an answer, Mohan burst into his best routine. He didn't have any music, but he never did in the forest. He kept his own music in his head. So he moved his feet and swung his hips and went wild. He boogied. He swayed. He shimmied. He pranced and strutted. There is an old saying: "Dance like no one is watching." And that's exactly what Mohan did.

It was an expression of pure joy, and the oni loved it. They all stopped their various tasks and howled and clapped and shouted watching Mohan dance!

"More! More!" they hollered.

"Thank you so much!" Mohan said. "I wish I could dance till dawn, but my parents will be worried, and I'm already well past my time. And I don't even have a full bucket of mushrooms to show for it, just a wet coat and tired legs. I had fun, but I can't do it again."

"If you can't dance again tonight, you must come tomorrow!" said the oni boss. "Promise us!"

Now Mohan thought of a proverb he had heard once. A wise man climbs Mount Fuji once, a fool twice. It seemed that dancing for the devils was brave the first time, and stupid the

second. So he did what he needed to do to get away. A little lie isn't always a bad thing…

"Of course I promise!" he replied, doing his best to look sincere.

"Yet you could speak falsely!" cried the oni boss. "You must leave us something valuable, a pledge for your return. Then we will believe you and trust you to come again and dance for us! What is the most valuable thing you own?"

Later he could never explain how his answer came to him. Call it inspiration. Call it pure luck. Sometimes you get a one-in-a-million idea just when you need it, and that was what happened right then. Mohan took a look at the red skin of the oni and he said with a straight face:

"See these red spots on my face?" Mohan said. "Human beings love them. They call them zits, and think the more spots you have, the more beautiful you are. If you take away all my zits, I will totally come back."

"Done!" shouted the oni boss. "A bargain struck!"

The oni boss stretched out his hand like he was grabbing something, and then closed it. Mohan felt a slight stinging in his face, and it was over. For the first time in his life, his face was smooth and clear. He ran straight home, where he told the whole story to his family. They were a good family, so they believed him.

The next day at school, Mohan was a wonder. Everyone wanted to know what had happened, and as much as he tried to play it cool he couldn't keep it in and eventually the story spread. Most didn't believe a word of it, but many did. After all, the evidence was right on Mohan's face! One person who absolutely believed it was Jessica. With Mohan's miraculous transformation she no longer had a target. Well, she figured, if it worked for Mohan it would work for her. That night she made up her mind to go into the woods, find the oni camp, and dance for them.

"You came back!" the oni shouted.

As Jessica made her way to the clearing, she saw the oni gathered around their fire. They had been waiting, excited for a repeat of last night. It might be strange to think that they didn't notice that this was a different person from the previous night, but they were oni after all—all humans looked the same to them. They didn't notice that Jessica wasn't Mohan, and if they did they didn't really care. They just wanted to see the dance again.

In her defense, Jessica did her best. But Jessica just couldn't dance like Mohan.

She tried to imitate dances she had seen on TV, but there was no music and Jessica didn't have the moves. She awkwardly stumbled across the forest floor. She waved her hands and even tried to sing along to give herself something to dance to. But it was hopeless. She was hopeless. It got so bad even the oni were embarrassed, staring at the ground, at the trees, at the fire, at anything to avoid the terrible scene before them.

"Enough!" said the oni boss

The oni boss (whose name was Toni, but that is neither here nor there), bellowed for Jessica to stop. By this time he had been desperately staring at the sky, trying to look at anything other than the stumbling girl. He sighed…

"You kept your promise and returned," he said. "And yet— alas! Whatever magic your dancing had must have been a trick of the moonlight. Or just luck on your part. I hate to put it so bluntly, but you are—terrible! We only ask that you never come here again! And we return your pledge, the pretty red spots that your kind values so much! Here they are back to you!"

With that said, Toni the oni (I promise that was his name!) stretched out his hand and held it before Jessica's face. She felt a painful sting, like her face was a hundred oil wells exploding at once. She didn't need a mirror to know what had happened. Instead of losing her own zits, she had added Mohan's.

The Woes of the ONYUDO

Knock, knock.

It wasn't the sort of thing Bahareh expected to hear in the late evening. Well, really, the timing wasn't so important—many people were out and about at night, and she was expecting a delivery. The real problem was that she lived on the second story, and no one should be knocking on her window.

Bahareh opened the shutters and looked outside; just as she suspected—a giant. Sigh… Recently, it was always a giant. What was worse, this was a one-eyed giant. The things you put up with in the modern world abroad. This sort of thing never happened at home.

"My name is Onyudo," bellowed the giant, "One eye have I! And stand as tall as the sky! Long have I walked and tired are my feet! Yet all would I endure to bring you this treat!"

To top it all off, he did an awkward dance while reciting his lines.

"Fine, fine," Bahareh sighed. She knew he was bucking for a tip with this performance. "Just hand over my kebab. And don't short me on the sauce like last time! I swear...I miss the old days when I had to walk downstairs to get my delivery. What if you had gotten my window wrong? GPS isn't magic, you know! You could have woken my neighbors with your tromping around! Anyways, just give me my kabab! And maybe your site should have a warning that a giant was going to deliver! I would've picked somewhere else!" The Onyudo shrugged his massive shoulders. The lady hadn't given much of a tip, but he wasn't expecting one. Life can be hard when you are thirty feet tall. He knew most people weren't happy when a giant showed up at their door, but what was he supposed to do? He was bald. He was a giant. He had one eye—pretty much all guarantees that he wasn't going to make many friends... He had hoped things would be different in this new city, that people would be more accepting, but not so much…

Oh well. Life goes on. And delivering kebab wasn't the worst job in the world. After all, there was always hope for something better. Even for one-eyed giants.

Maybe especially for one-eyed giants.

Quinn & the
TANUKI DANCE

QUINN AND HENRY WERE HEADING HOME FROM PRACTICE when they heard the sound. They were walking through the forest, as they had done for months. But tonight, instead of the usual bird-songs and whispering wind they were used to, they heard something odd.

The first thing they noticed was the thrum thrum thrum of the drums. It wasn't the usual sound of drums—they could hear that there was something more going on than the sound of mallets pounding against stretched skins. There was something magical about the thrum-thrum-thrumming.

Pom-poko-pom-poko-pom

"We have to go look," Quinn said. He was already on his

way towards the music. It was hypnotic. Every stroke of the drum called to him. His feet were tapping. There were voices, too—it sounded like a party.

"No way!" said Henry. "We're supposed to go straight home after practice! Our moms said so."

"Well yeah," Quinn said, "but they didn't know we would find something cool. We have to at least go check it out. Sure, we'll be home a little late, but…don't you want to see? It sounds fun! A festival!"

"Fine," Henry huffed. He liked to obey the rules, and it made him feel very uncomfortable to go against plans. Quinn and he had decided what time they would leave practice, what route they would take home, and what time they would arrive. It was a good plan. They shouldn't be distracted by some drumming. But still… he wanted to know too…

"Come on!" Quinn was dragging Henry. He pushed their way through the bushes, heading towards a glimmering light they could see in the distance. Parting the brush, they could see lanterns being hung from the trees, and the magical creatures called tanuki assembling for a party. The mood was festive. And fun…

Pom-poko-pom-poko-pom

"We gotta go home," said Henry. "We're not supposed to be here. I don't feel good about this at all—we shouldn't even be seeing this! I mean, look at them! They're animals! Yokai! We have to go home…we have a curfew!"

"I know. But honestly, I think our parents would understand. These are tanuki! Dancing! How many chances in our life are we going to get to do something like this? I think…I think you take your chances when they come. I think I have to go for it."

"Fine," said Henry. "But I'm going home like we're supposed to." With that he went back to the road and made his way home, leaving Quinn behind.

Pom-poko-pom-poko-pom

Quinn parted the plants that kept him from the festival, and stepped into the circle. He looked cautiously at the party. When the yokai noticed him, they called to him.

Quinn spent the rest of the night dancing it up with tanuki. It was awesome.

The Tengu &
THE BIRDS

THE TENGU SAT QUIETLY ON A MOUNTAINTOP, when he was joined by a pair of birds. It seemed like the perfect opportunity to ask some questions about things that had been troubling him lately. He knew that birds were often wise and he could trust their answers.

"Hello, birds," said the tengu. "If I may be so rude as to ask a question: Why do you fly?"

The birds rustled their feathers, and settled in on their branches. They knew an important conversation was coming.

"We fly because we are birds," they said. "It is in our nature to do so."

"I see," said the tengu. "And why do you sit on branches?"

"Again, because we are birds," they replied. "Were we fish, we would live in the water and swim. Were we people, we would live in houses and ride in vehicles. But we are birds. So we fly and sit on branches. We eat worms and do other bird things. Squawk and squabble."

"Do you never swim?" asked the tengu. "Or ride in vehicles?"

"Never."

"Do you dance?"

"Well…yes," said the birds. "Sometimes. As the mood strikes us. Birds can also dance."

Hearing this the Tengu stroked his long nose, and pondered. The answers to his questions had only led to more questions.

"So what am I?" asked the tengu. "I have feathers and wings—I am bird-like, but not a bird. I have arms and legs—I am human-like, yet not one of their kind. I can fly. I can walk. I can ride in vehicles (although I choose not to). So what is correct for me? Which is my nature? What should I be?"

"Why," the bird said, nestling even deeper in her own feathers, "you should be who you are."

"And how do I do that?" he said. "How do I know what is myself?"

"No one can tell you who you are, but you," answered the birds, smartly. "If you are not one thing or another thing, then you must be the thing you are. As to what that is—you already know. Be the thing you are."

"I see," said the tengu, satisfied.

"And one more thing."

"Yes?"

"Don't look to us for answers," they said. "We're just a couple of birds."

The tengu smiled at that. He then pulled out his flute, and began to play a jaunty tune.

The birds danced.

Nº 15

Tsukumogami
BIRTHDAY

IT WASN'T THE USUAL MOOD FOR A BIRTHDAY PARTY; but then again it wasn't a usual birthday party. If you could even call it that—it was more like a "hopefully-a-birthday party," because those at the party were hoping something would be born. Late at night, the tsukumogami gathered, huddled around something that looked like an old leather box with knobs.

"I feel good about this one," said the kasa obake, an ancient umbrella wagging a huge red tongue. It hopped around on a single foot, and had one giant eye that never blinked.

"You've ssssaid that about the lassst sssseventy…" whispered ittan momen, a wisp of cloth that was centuries old but still white and fresh as the day it was woven. "But none of them came to life.

It is sssstill jusssst usssss."

"Now, now!" They all stopped their chatting when seto taisho, the dinnerware general, began to speak. He tapped his needle sword across his china-pot chest with a clink clink clink, calling the group to order. "We've had a lot of letdowns recently, too many birthday parties where nothing was born. But we can't give up on hope. We tsukumogami are some of the oldest yokai. It's in our nature to last."

"But there are fewer us born every year!" This sound came from the ceiling, where the bake chochin, the yokai lantern, hovered above them all. Its single eye and red tongue made it the cousin of the kasa obake.

"It takes a hundred years for something to become a tsukumogami!" the bake chochin said. "Modern things just aren't made to last! They break, they fall apart… When's the last time you've seen a pair of shoes last a hundred years! Or a coffee mug? Or a…a…lantern! I don't think they even make lanterns anymore!"

"I think we all know how it works, but just in case," said the dinnerware general. "An object one hundred years old can come to life, but not just any object. Something that was made of excellent quality; something that has been used and useful for a hundred years. Collector's items wrapped in plastic cases—

pots and plates and objects sitting in museums—they will never become tsukumogami. It takes a hundred years of human affection to put a soul into a lifeless object. Each hand that touches us adds a bit of life."

"And yes, there are fewer of us each year," said seto taisho. "Some tsukumogami get tired, or break. Some just fade away, and fewer new ones are being born. Things are disposable nowadays. People barely plan for five years, much less a hundred. And they get bored of their stuff. Or it falls out of fashion, and then it is off to the trash heap! But we tsukumogami are special for a reason—we are masterpieces, works of practical art. Humankind is never done with art. And so there will always be new tsukumogami. There just may be…fewer of us, as time goes by. But few is not nothing. So let us hope together."

"Almost time," said seto taisho. "Fingers crossed everyone, if you have them. Fingers, that is…"

This was a bigger hopefully-a-birthday party than any of them wanted to admit. The box they were huddled around was not just a box—it was an old Victrola radio, lovingly maintained by a gentle man who had passed it down to his great granddaughter Anna. She was enchanted by it, and listened to it night after night for most of her life, twisting the dials and gleefully tuning in to whatever the old radio station could pick up. She

liked that it was old. She liked that it still worked. She used it and loved it—and possibly that was enough.

If so, it would be something completely new—the first electric tsukumogami. Since the dawn of electricity there had been fewer and fewer tsukumogami. Electronic devices were not built to last. But there was an exception or two, and maybe this was one of them. And maybe, just maybe, that would mean hope for the future.

The clock ticked. The whole world seemed to be holding its breath. The cloth yokai ittan momen twisted its own tail. The kasa obake and obake chochin huddled close together. The dinnerware general seto taisho stood rigid like a leader should, but inside he was shaking. As the ticks of the clock moved time forward, the weathered old radio turned exactly one hundred years old. It was time…

"Sssseee. I told you. It'sss hopelesss…" whispered ittan momen.

"Hu…hu…hullo?" The voice sounded unsure. It was accompanied by the creaks of leather as once-lifeless material reshaped itself into a mouth. Static blasted as the knobs moved on their own. One-hundred-year-old wood and cardboard reinvigorated.

"N…nice to m…meet you all," said the radio. "What's happening? Why are you here? And…who am I?"

"Bake radio…" The little dinnerware general was so moved,

he dropped his needle sword. "Y…your name is bake radio. And we are very, very happy to meet you."

Everyone shouted together:

"Happy Birthday!"

Anna & the
WANYUDO

"COME ON ANNA! You heard your mother. Get over here and help." Her dad was smiling, but you could tell there was an edge in his voice. He was honestly worried.

"You know there is a forecast for a Wanyudo in town tonight," he said. "We have to cover up the windows. After all, you don't want to be seen, do you? "

"Right, Dad," Anna chided. "A flaming monk's head, stuck on a wagon wheel, is going to come roaming through town, and whoever it sees dies…this is just the stupidest superstition. At least the Easter Bunny brings chocolate and candy!"

"This isn't quite the same thing as the Easter Bunny," her dad said, tensely. "I know you think it seems silly, but just do it, okay?"

"Mom, why do you even believe this kind of thing?" Anna said. "Aren't you a scientist?"

Mariko smiled at her daughter, and looked loving at her husband Akira. Things do come full circle, it seems.

"Listen Anna," Mariko said. "My own mother told me something once, and now I'll pass it on to you. The world doesn't always make sense. Sometimes things are mysterious, and you can't understand them. You just accept them. You allow yourself to be amazed, and maybe a little scared, but you don't try to look for answers."

"And that's it, huh?"

"That's it."

"Fiiiiine."

Anna grabbed some blankets and helped fix them around the windows with the rest of her family. Wanyudo nights were supposed to be scary, but…she'd never admit it, but it was fun, doing this every now and then. They'd hang the blankets, then light candles and make hot amazake sweet drinks, and huddle together and laugh.

It wasn't bad, Anna thought. After all, even the most skeptical person needs to leave a little room in their life for magic.

And monsters…

And yokai…

☞ The Authors

ELEONORA D'ONOFRIO is a Swiss/Italian illustrator and 3D artist working in England. The experiences she's had whilst living abroad have influenced her work and taste for art, from Japan's love of simplicity to Italian Classics. Before specialising in 3D she published with several independent Italian Magazines (*Canemarcio*, *La Legione degli Artisti*), with illustrators she met while studying in Bologna. Currently her work is mostly computer based graphics but whenever possible she reverts back to her favourite medium: acrylics and pencil.

ZACK DAVISSON is an award-winning translator, writer, and folklorist. He wrote *Yurei: The Japanese Ghost*, *Kaibyo: The Supernatural Cats of Japan*, and translated Shigeru Mizuki's *Kitaro* and Go Nagai's *Devilman*. Davisson lectured on translation and folklore at Duke, UCLA, University of Washington, and contributed to Wereldmuseum Rotterdam. He was nominated for the Japanese-US Friendship Translation Prize for the Eisner Award-winning *Showa: A History of Japan*. He lives in Seattle, Washington, with wife Miyuki, a dog, two cats, and several ghosts.